To Babcia,

Thank you for loving me unconditionally, for always believing in me, and for helping to walk me home.

— J.M.

TROLLEY STOP
PUBLISHING

Copyright © 2025 by Trolley Stop Publishing
8677 Villa La Jolla Drive #898
La Jolla, CA 92037

All rights reserved. No portion of this book may be reproduced in any form without permission from the publisher, except as permitted by U.S. copyright law in articles and reviews.
For permissions visit www.JohnMasiulionis.com.

Publisher's Cataloging-in-Publication Data

Names: Masiulionis, John, Author. | Barwinska, Roksana, Illustrator.
Title: Walking Each Other Home — Zachary's Mission: A Hospice for Children / Written by John Masiulionis; Illustrated by Roksana Barwinska.
Description: La Jolla, CA: Trolley Stop Publishing, 2025. | Summary: With help from several Earth Angels, Zachary, a boy with cancer, accomplishes his final mission: to build a children's hospice in La Jolla, California.
Identifiers: LCCN: 2023919707 | ISBN: 979-8-9919306-0-4 (hardcover)
Subjects: LCSH Hospices (Terminal care)--Juvenile fiction. | Cancer--Juvenile fiction. | Children and death--Juvenile fiction. | Terminally ill--Juvenile fiction. | La Jolla (San Diego, Calif.)--Juvenile fiction. | BISAC JUVENILE FICTION / Health & Daily Living / Diseases, Illnesses & Injuries | JUVENILE FICTION / Social Themes / Death, Grief, Bereavement
Classification: LCC PZ7.1 .M37 Wa 2025 | DDC [E]--dc23

Zachary's Mission: A Hospice for Children

Written by
John Masiulionis

Illustrated by
Roksana Barwinska

Poor Zachary has been feeling sick lately, so Dr. Robinson wanted to run some tests. Zachary's big sister, Kristen, is worried, so Zachary holds her hand. Visiting the doctor can be scary sometimes!

Dr. Robinson does not have good news. The whole family listens as he explains that Zachary has cancer.

"Is there anything we can do?" asks Zachary's dad.

Dr. Robinson sighs but says kindly, "Unfortunately, not much."

Zachary is confused. "What is cancer?"

Dr. Robinson replies, "Zachary, cancer is an illness that affects your whole body. You'll feel tired, sad, and maybe even angry sometimes.

Your cancer is terminal, meaning we can't cure it, but we'll do our best to help you feel better. We'll see each other often, so you can ask me anything you're concerned about."

Zachary's mom pulls him close. "Dad and I will be right here, supporting you the whole time."

"Me too!" adds Kristen.

Back home, Kristen has a surprise for Zachary. She presents him with a very special notebook.

"What is this for?" asks Zachary.

"Mom and Dad are worried about you, so I got you a journal you can use to express your emotions any way you like – but only if you want to!"

Kristen gives her little brother a big, squishy hug, and Zachary hugs her right back.

"Thanks, Sis. I love it!"

Later that night, Zachary gazes at the sky filled with shining stars and a big bright moon. He decides to go out into the yard for a better look. Somehow being under that moon after such an upsetting day makes him want to talk to God.

He closes his eyes and begins to pray. "God, I hope you can hear me. I'm a little scared. Could you help me be brave? Also, could you please send strength to my parents? I don't like seeing them so sad. I really appreciate it. Thank you. Amen."

While sleeping snuggled safely in his bed, Zachary has a visitor.

"God, is that *really* You?"

God smiles and says, "Yes, little one. I heard your prayer, and I understand that you are scared. I came to give you an important mission."

"A mission?" Zachary asks him.

"Yes," God says. "I want you to create a hospice for you and children like yourself. A hospice is a place where those with terminal illnesses can pass away peacefully. This hospice will be unique as sick children can have their final dreams come true."

Zachary is excited and nervous. "That sounds like an amazing plan. But why me? What if I mess up?"

God chuckles. "You are the perfect person for this mission, Zachary! You are one of the bravest souls I know.

You have empathy, compassion, and understanding of others. The love in your heart is as vast as an ocean. There is no one else like you! Believe in yourself because you are special just as you are. Come with me. I want to show you something."

In a flash, Zachary finds himself in a room unlike any he has ever seen before.

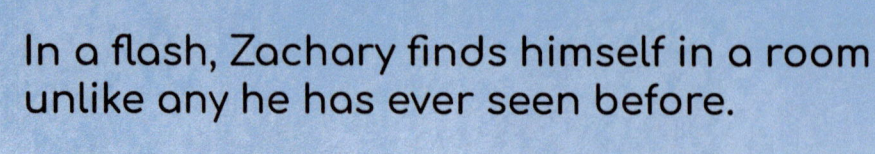

God smiles at Zachary. "You won't be alone; you'll have plenty of support. Here are the four Earth Angels to help you with your mission. Meet Jane, Dennis, Georgeanne, and Patrick. I chose each one specifically to help you bring love and happiness into the lives of the children that will stay in the hospice and to their families."

"This is Jane. She shows her love by taking care of and spending quality time with her grandchildren."

Zachary stares intently at Jane surrounded by her grandchildren. "I can show love to others by spending time with them?"

God smiles and says, "Absolutely you can. Think of it this way: You could be doing something else, but you set aside time for the ones you love instead. That creates treasured memories and moments to cherish for a lifetime."

"Next is Dennis, the owner of a popular Italian restaurant. Dennis shows his love by feeding those who are hungry."

Zachary nods. "His way of showing love is making people a nice warm meal."

"Exactly, Zachary. Food tastes better when it's shared!"

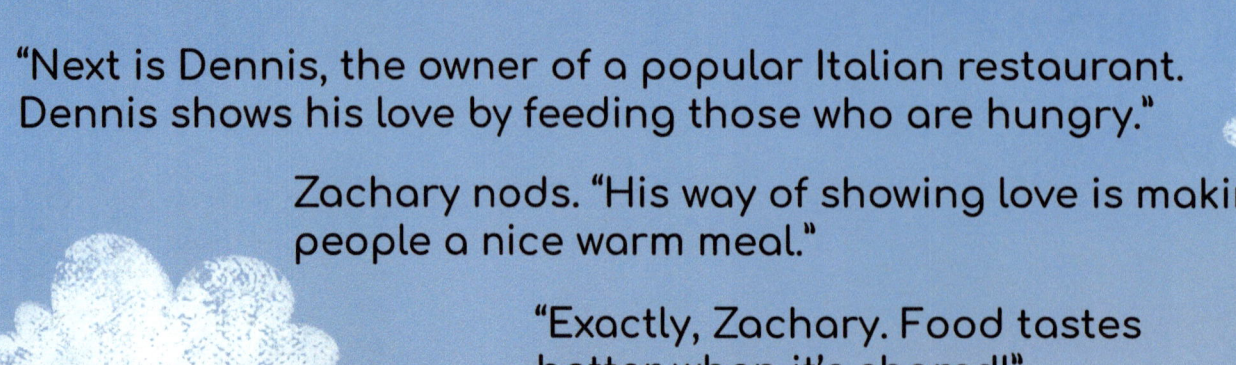

God points to the next screen. "This is your third Earth Angel, Georgeanne. She shows her devotion to our animal friends by sharing their stories with children."

"You picked her because she shows compassion and kindness to all creatures, right?" Zachary grins.

God answers, "That is correct."

"We need more people like that in the world."

"We certainly do."

"And lastly, here's Patrick, a Reiki Master. Patrick is showing his love by helping people to feel better."

"How does he do that?" Zachary asks.

"He uses Reiki, a spiritual healing technique that helps people relax. It also reduces stress and anxiety."

"Wow! That is super cool!" Zachary says.

"Super cool indeed," replies God.

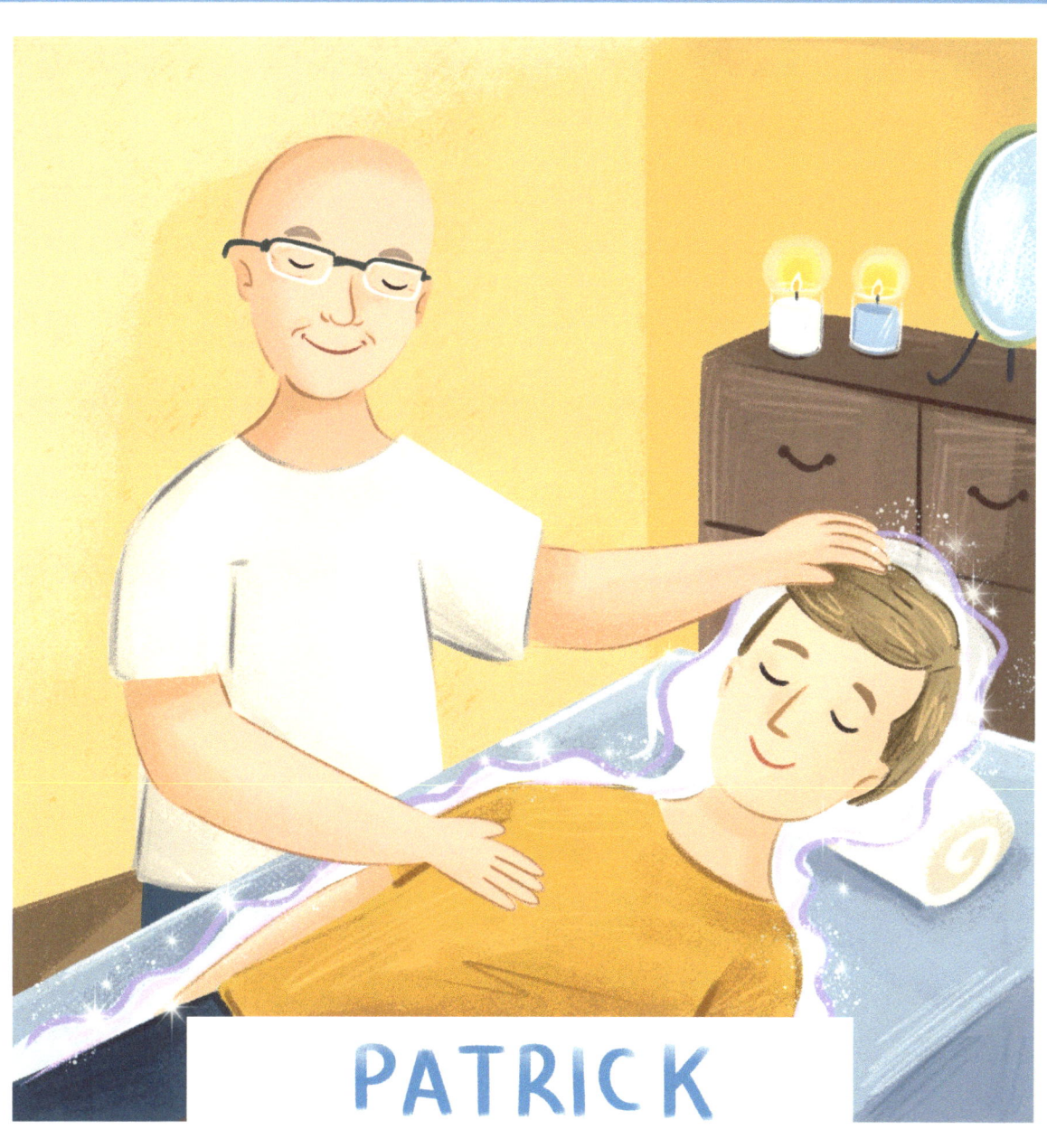

Suddenly Zachary is awakened by his laptop. Someone is trying to reach him. Who could it be?

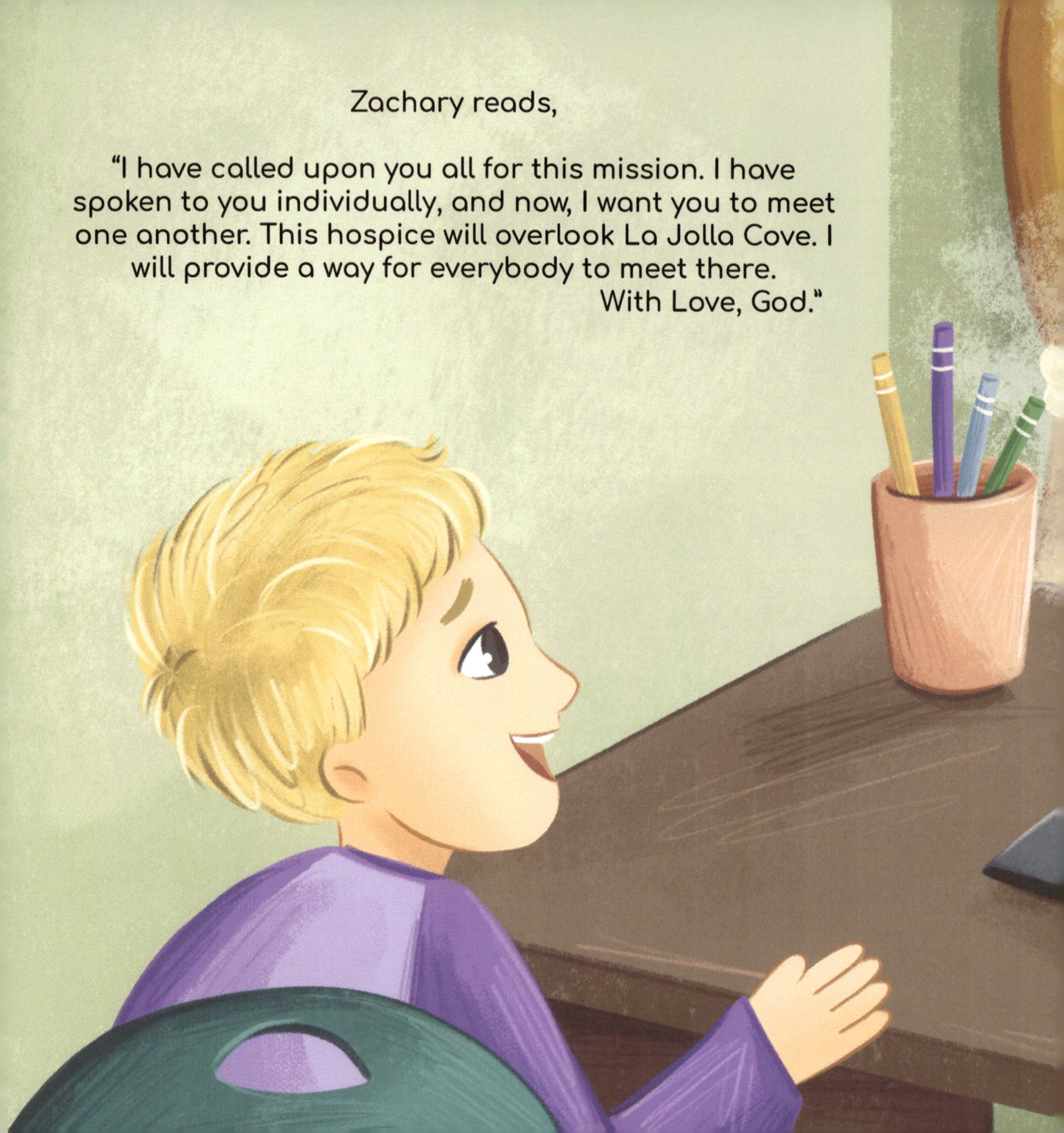

Zachary reads,

"I have called upon you all for this mission. I have spoken to you individually, and now, I want you to meet one another. This hospice will overlook La Jolla Cove. I will provide a way for everybody to meet there.
With Love, God."

"God, trust in me. I can do this!"

The Earth Angels gather in San Diego to help Zachary with his mission. They are excited to fulfill God's plan and head directly to Zachary's house to meet.

"It must be very hard for Zachary, having a terminal diagnosis," says Jane.

"Yes, Zachary is dying, but he has a purpose and a goal. The mission is to make that happen and support him along the way," Dennis affirms.

Zachary and his family are so happy to meet the Earth Angels that God chose to help him.

"Thank you all for trusting in God and me," says Zachary with a big smile.

Together they discuss all the many ways they can raise funds. They have so many ideas and are ready to begin!

Georgeanne and Patrick work together to get support from the community.

Georgeanne beams and says, "I shop here all the time, so I know many people. We should be able to get lots of signatures and donations."

"Wonderful! Have you invited your friends?" Patrick asks.

"I have and they are out getting donations right now!" Georgeanne says excitedly.

"That is great! We'll reach our goal soon!" says Patrick confidently.

Jane and Dennis visit a local restaurant together. "I did some research and already spoke with the owner. They are willing to help us get donations. It's incredible!" exclaims Dennis.

"Are we meeting the owner here?"

"We are," replies Dennis. "Also, he wants to give us a list of people who can help spread the word. He suggested starting with Dr. Glenn, a beloved chiropractor."

"That is so thoughtful. The list will definitely help. Let's find Dr. Glenn."

At Dr Glenn's office, Dennis introduces everyone.

"Dr. Glenn," Zachary says, "thank you so much for your time. We need donations to build a children's hospice, for terminal kids like me. It will be a really special place to spend time with our families before we go home to God."

Dr. Glenn smiles. "I would be honored to help. I can call a friend of mine, Wayne, who is an audio technician from Pittsburgh. He is visiting San Diego right now, and I know he would be happy to assist."

"Thanks, Dr. Glenn! We appreciate your help," Zachary says, with his heart filled with hope.

With his family's encouragement, Zachary goes online to ask for support with his mission. He has never been in a live video before, so he's a little nervous, but he's also brave and knows God will help him.

"Thank you to everyone joining us. We need help getting the word out about a hospice we want to build in La Jolla, the jewel of San Diego. It's a place for sick kids from all over the country who need a safe and loving place while they go through what can be a very hard time. Hospice is a place to be cared for, and to make wonderful memories, even while you are really sick. I will need hospice care soon. That's why I am talking to you guys, so we can reach our goal. It will take a lot of money and a lot of support."

Kristen adds, "Please, if you can, donate to this worthy cause. My little brother is the bravest person I know and a real hero!"

LIVE

"Look!" Zachary shouts. "The numbers keep going up!"

Everyone gathers as the donations pour in and cheers excitedly as they finally reach their goal.

Zachary closes his eyes and says, "God has provided."

GOAL!
YOU ARE STRONG! -ERIN
YOU ARE SPECIAL! -DAVID
NEVER GIVE UP! -DR. GLENN
YOU ARE LOVED! -WAYNE

Shortly after the group reaches their goal, construction on the hospice begins. Zachary, his family, and the Earth Angels are first on site to help.

Zachary sighs, proud and at peace. "We did it! I'm so glad God answered my prayer! It's not easy being sick or in pain, but with everyone's help, we made it happen."

"It's important that you talk about your struggles," says Zachary's dad, "because I know that expressing our emotions and feeling our feelings can make challenging situations much more manageable."

"I know," Zachary replies, "and being able to talk to everyone about my feelings has helped me to remember I'm not alone."

Finally, the hospice is complete. Sick children and their families can now move in and experience the beauty, joy, and peacefulness that God planned for them. It's time for the opening ceremony. It seems everyone in town has come to celebrate!

Zachary knows he could not have fulfilled his mission without help from God, his family, and the Earth Angels. It was a real team effort!

Before his speech, Zachary pauses and tunes into his heart before reciting, "Love is both patient and kind. It always protects. Love is hopeful, trusting, and always persevering. Love never fails, and it never dies. It only changes form. We are all here to help walk each other home."

Then Zachary cuts the ribbon, and everyone cheers.

"Here, Sis. I want you to have this," Zachary says as he hands Kristen the journal she gave him.

"But why? This was *my* gift to you."

"Now it's my gift to you. I filled it full of memories, starting from the day you gave it to me, until this morning. I wanted you to have something to remember me by. Just know, I'll be watching over you when I'm in Heaven."

Zachary has another journal, as well. "And this one is for when you feel sad. Writing helped me. It will help you too."

Kristen smiles. "You're the best. I love you."

"Ditto!" Zachary replies cheerfully.

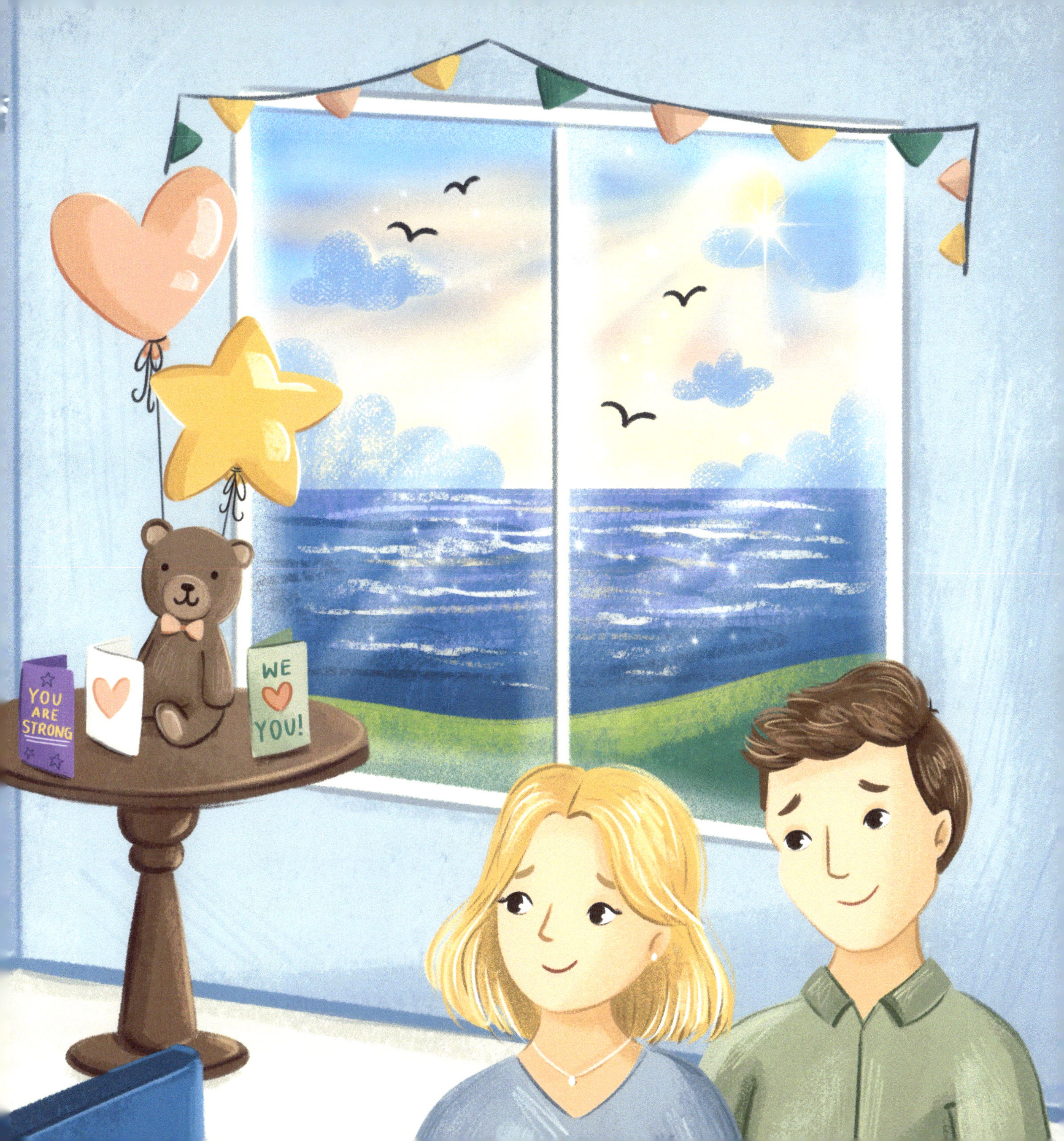
YOU ARE STRONG
WE ♥ YOU!

"God, this is the proudest I have ever been in my whole life. I'm so happy to know that my mission is complete. Now other children will have a peaceful place to stay before going to Heaven. They even get to meet people they really admire! I have seen children's authors, musicians, and even professional wrestlers visiting children and their families. I really hope you can help my family feel the love I will always have for them, even when I am no longer here. God, I know I'm ready now."

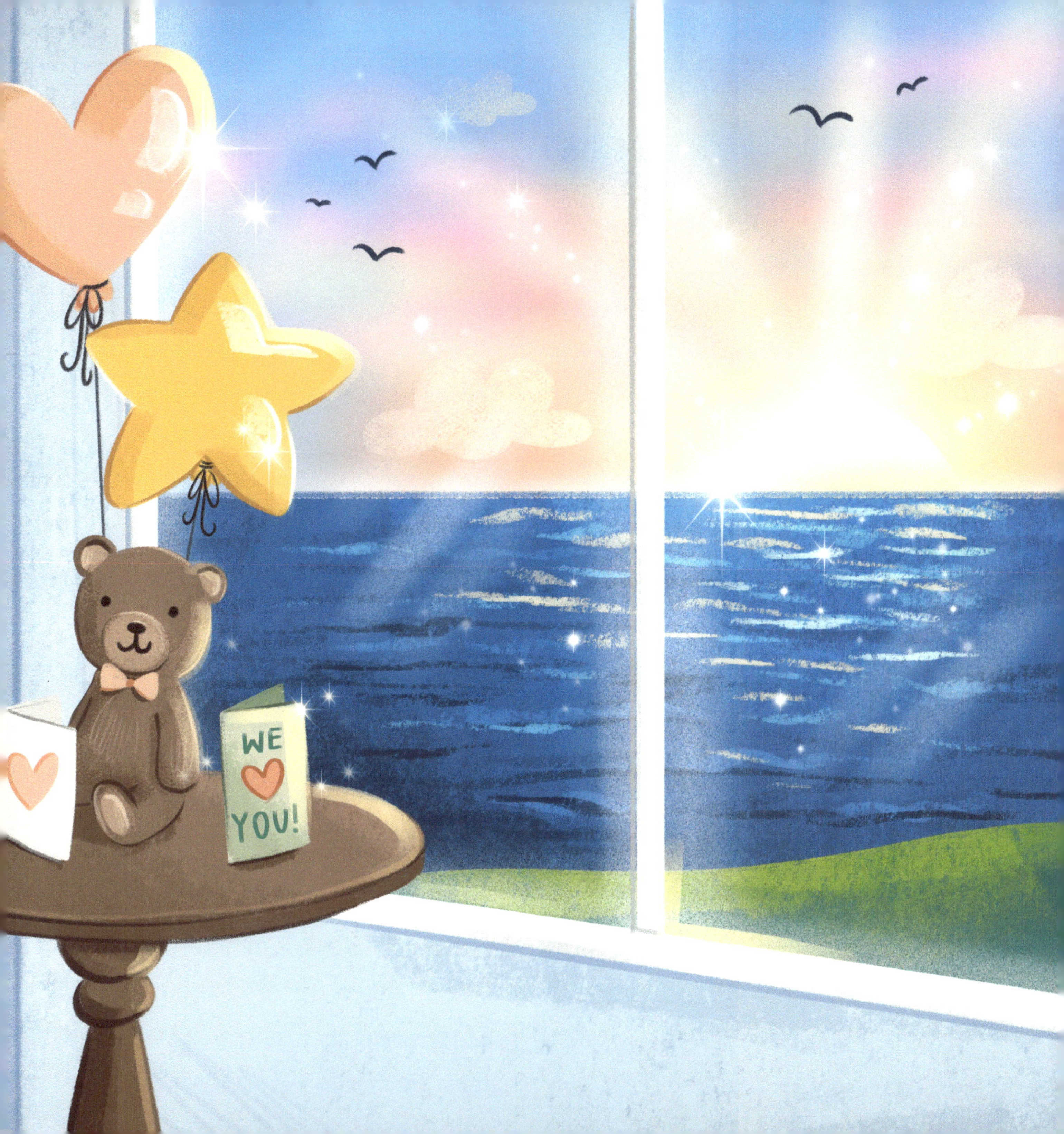
WE
YOU!

It's time for Zachary to go home to Heaven. Everyone is with him and surrounding him with their love. They take comfort knowing Zachary is no longer in pain, and that he will be safe in Heaven. It hurts to say goodbye, but they remember what Zachary courageously taught them . . .

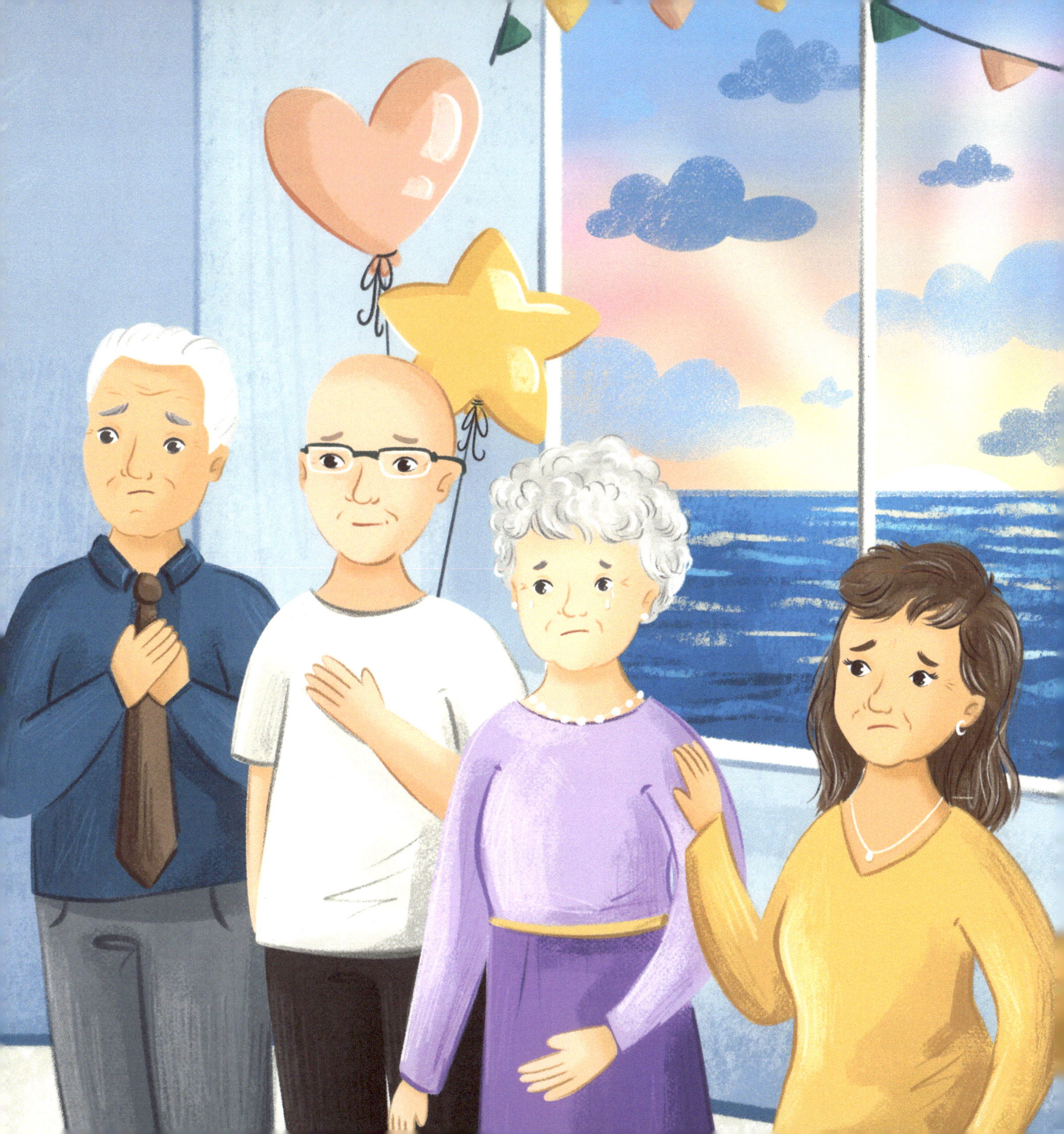

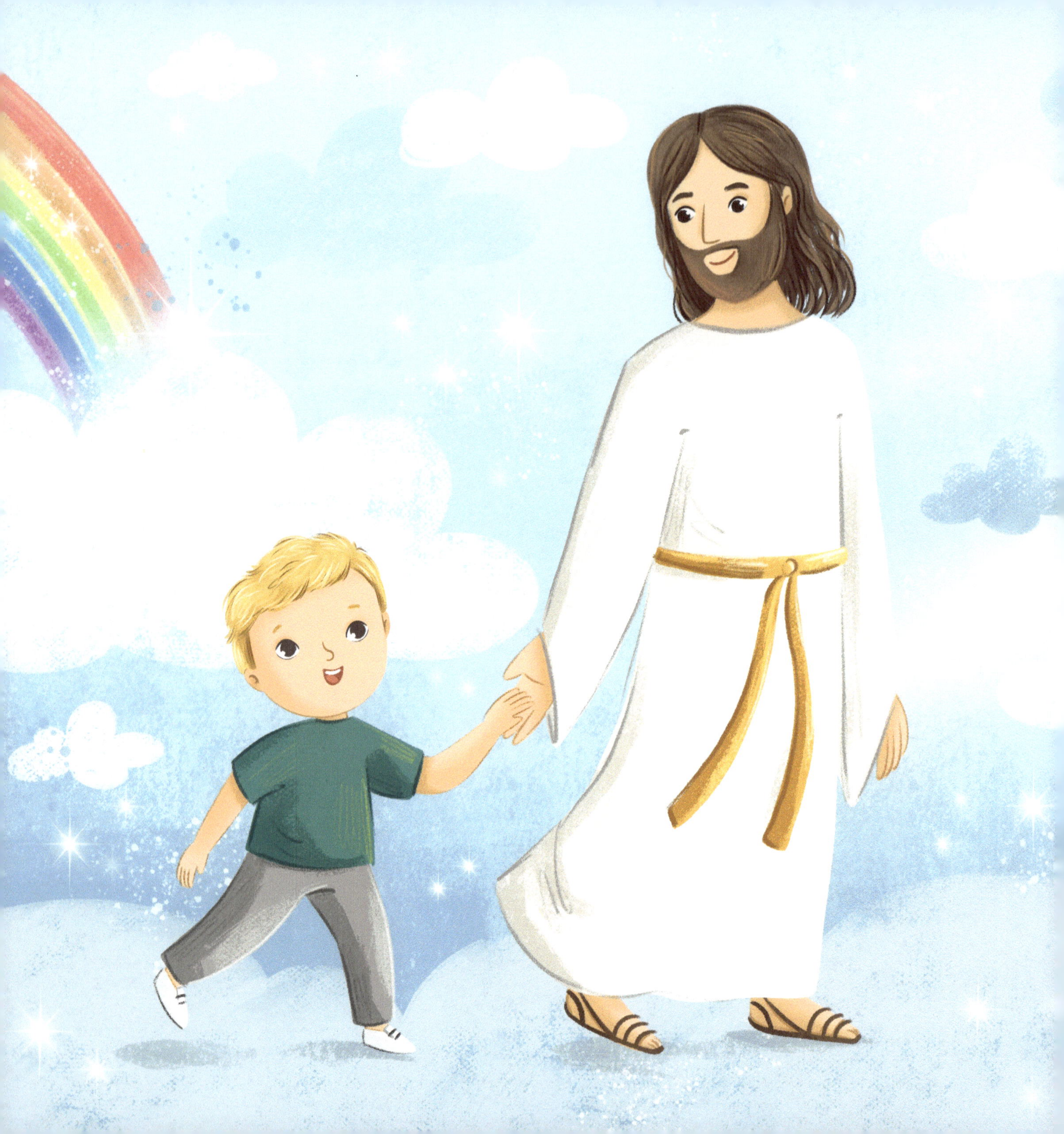

"Love never dies – It only changes form."

About the Author

John Masiulionis is a debut children's author, founder of PR From The Heart, a leading KidLit public relations firm, and host of The Children's Books Spotlight Series, one of the longest-running podcasts in the world of children's literature. With a passion for storytelling and a desire to help children and their families navigate life's toughest challenges, he wrote Walking Each Other Home — Zachary's Mission: A Hospice for Children. John's work is inspired by the memory of his late grandmother, as well as his time connecting hospitalized children with professional wrestlers while hosting the award-winning radio show, Monday Night Mayhem. He resides in San Diego with his beloved Shih Tzu/Maltese, Little Forrest.

JohnMasiulionis.com

About the Illustrator

Roksana Barwinska is a children's illustrator based in Poland. She has illustrated picture books, educational books, and board games for clients around the world. Roksana works digitally and loves to create playful and colorful illustrations, with a pinch of magic.

RoksanaBarwinska.com

Sincerest gratitude goes out to Donna, Rebecca, Megan, Roksana, Brooke, and Allie. For years, this book was only a vision in my mind's eye. With your tireless efforts, your thoughtful time and care, and the sharing of your gifts, that vision has now become a reality. And for that, I am deeply grateful.

A special shout-out to John Parra, one of KidLit's brightest stars. You saw a spark in me years ago and knew that I had a story to share with the world. I am truly thankful for your unwavering belief in me. Your confidence in my abilities has been a constant source of strength.

A speedy thank you to David Newell. I never would have thought in a million years that the beloved Mr. McFeely on Mister Rogers' Neighborhood would become a dear friend, a trusted neighbor, and a fellow KidLit advocate. I appreciate the gift of your friendship, which I will forever cherish.

To the heaven-sent helpers on my path, Dennis, Georgeanne, and Patrick: The three of you, along with my grandmother, are shining examples of what it means to be real-life Earth Angels. Your support means more to me than you will ever know.

And last, but not least, a heartfelt hug to Little Forrest. You are my pride and joy. Thank you for being my faithful furry friend and forever companion in this journey called life. I love you, little guy.

Author visits are available for your class, school, group, or organization. For more information, visit JohnMasiulionis.com or connect with John on social media @JohnMasiulionis.